SECRET AGENT

JACK
STALWART

Peril at the
Grand Prix:
ITALY

Join Secret Agent Jack Stalwart

on his other adventures:

The Search for the Sunken Treasure: **AUSTRALIA**

The Secret of the Sacred Temple: **CAMBODIA**

The Puzzle of the Missing Panda: **CHINA**

The Mystery of the Mona Lisa: **FRANCE**

The Caper of the Crown Jewels: **GREAT BRITAIN**

The Pursuit of the Ivory Poachers: **KENYA**

The Escape of the Deadly Dinosaur: **USA**

Peril
at the
Grand Prix:
ITALY

Elizabeth Singer Hunt

Illustrated by Brian Williamson

RED FOX

PERIL AT THE GRAND PRIX: ITALY
A RED FOX BOOK 978 1 862 30473 4

First published in Great Britain by Red Fox,
an imprint of Random House Children's Books
A Random House Group Company

This edition published 2007

Text copyright © Elizabeth Singer Hunt, 2007
Illustrations copyright © Brian Williamson, 2007, adapted from the original
Jack Stalwart illustrations © Elizabeth Singer Hunt, 2004–5

The Random House Group Limited makes every effort to ensure that the papers used
in its books are from trees that have been legally sourced from well-managed and
credibly certified forests. Our paper procurement policy can be found at
www.randomhouse.co.uk/paper.htm

Set in Meta, Trixie, American Typewriter, Luggagetag, Gill Sans Condensed and
Serpentine.

Red Fox Books are published by Random House Children's Books,
61–63 Uxbridge Road, London W5 5SA

www.kidsatrandomhouse.co.uk

Addresses for companies within The Random House Group Limited can be found at:
www.randomhouse.co.uk/offices.htm

THE RANDOM HOUSE GROUP Limited Reg. No. 954009

A CIP catalogue record for this book is available from the British Library.

Printed in the UK by CPI Bookmarque, Croydon, CR0 4TD

*For Morgan, who
loves cars 'so, so much'*

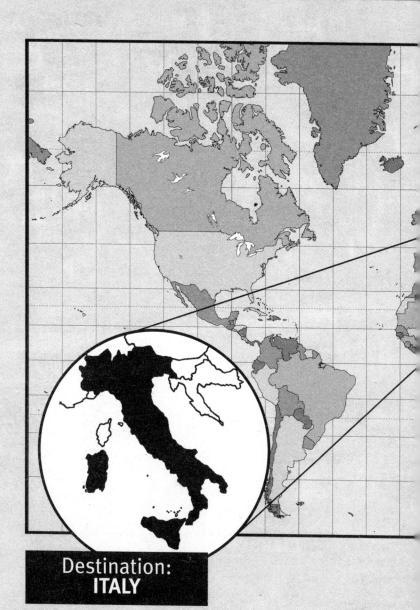

Destination:
ITALY

My name is Jack Stalwart. My older brother,
Max, was a secret agent for you, until he
disappeared on one of your missions. Now I
want to be a secret agent too. If you choose
me, I will be an excellent secret agent and get
rid of evil villains, just like my brother did.
Sincerely,

Jack Stalwart

Jack Stalwart was sworn in as a Global
Protection Force secret agent four months ago.
Since that time, he has completed all of his
missions successfully and has stopped no less
than twelve evil villains. Because of this he
has been assigned the code name 'COURAGE'.

Jack has yet to uncover the whereabouts of
his brother, Max, who is still working for this
organization at a secret location. Do not give
Secret Agent Jack Stalwart this information.
He is never to know about his brother.

Gerald Barter

Gerald Barter
Director, Global Protection Force

THINGS YOU'LL FIND IN EVERY BOOK

Watch Phone: The only gadget Jack wears all the time, even when he's not on official business. His Watch Phone is the central gadget that makes most others work. There are lots of important features, most importantly the 'C' button, which reveals the code of the day – necessary to unlock Jack's Secret Agent Book Bag. There are buttons on both sides, one of which ejects his life-saving Melting Ink Pen. Beyond these functions, it also works as a phone and, of course, gives Jack the time of day.

Global Protection Force (GPF): The GPF is the organization Jack works for. It's a worldwide force of young secret agents whose aim is to protect the world's people, places and possessions. No one knows exactly where its main offices are located (all correspondence and gadgets for repair are sent to a special PO Box, and training is held at various locations around the world), but Jack thinks it's somewhere cold, like the Arctic Circle.

Whizzy: Jack's magical miniature globe. Almost every night at precisely 7:30 p.m., the GPF uses Whizzy to send Jack the identity of the country that he must travel to. Whizzy can't talk, but he can cough up messages. Jack's parents don't know Whizzy is anything more than a normal globe.

The Magic Map: The magical map hanging on Jack's bedroom wall. Unlike most maps, the GPF's map is made of a mysterious wood. Once Jack inserts the country piece from Whizzy, the map swallows Jack whole and sends him away on his missions. When he returns, he arrives precisely one minute after he left.

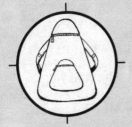

Secret Agent Book Bag: The Book Bag that Jack wears on every adventure. Licensed only to GPF secret agents, it contains top-secret gadgets necessary to foil bad guys and escape certain death. To activate the bag before each mission, Jack must punch in a secret code given to him by his Watch Phone. Once he's away, all he has to do is place his finger on the zip, which identifies him as the owner of the bag and immediately opens.

THE STALWART FAMILY

Jack's dad, John

He moved the family to England when Jack was two, in order to take a job with an aerospace company. As far as Jack knows, his dad designs and manufactures aeroplane parts. Jack's dad thinks he is an ordinary boy and that his other son, Max, attends a school in Switzerland. Jack's dad is American and his mum is British, which makes Jack a bit of both.

Jack's mum, Corinne

One of the greatest mums as far as Jack is concerned. When she and her husband received a letter from a posh school in Switzerland inviting Max to attend, they were overjoyed. Since Max left six months ago, they have received numerous notes in Max's handwriting telling them he's OK. Little do they know it's all a lie and that it's the GPF sending those letters.

Jack's older brother, Max

Two years ago, at the age of nine, Max joined the GPF. Max used to tell Jack about his adventures and show him how to work his secret-agent gadgets. When the family received a letter inviting Max to attend a school in Europe, Jack figured it was to do with the GPF. Max told him he was right, but that he couldn't tell Jack anything about why he was going away.

Nine-year-old Jack Stalwart

Four months ago, Jack received an anonymous note saying: 'Your brother is in danger. Only you can save him.' As soon as he could, Jack applied to be a secret agent too. Since that time, he's battled some of the world's most dangerous villains, and hopes some day in his travels to find and rescue his brother, Max.

DESTINATION:
Italy

Italy is called
'*il Belpaese*', or
'Beautiful Country'

•

Rome is its capital city

•

Today, over 58 million
people live in Italy

•

The country is divided
into twenty regions,
including Tuscany
and Sardinia

The Leaning Tower of
Pisa is located in the
north of the country.
It was built over 800
years ago

•

The Vatican City,
the Pope's 'home', is
located in Rome

•

The Italian national
football team has won
the World Cup four
times (1934, 1938, 1982
and 2006) in Rome

MOTOR RACING: FACTS AND FIGURES

The world's first racing car was called a De Dion

Built in 1884 by the French, the De Dion had four wheels, no steering wheel and was powered by steam. It could reach a top speed of 35 miles per hour

During the 1890s, cars with petrol engines were introduced

The first proper race between petrol-powered cars and steam-powered engines was called the Paris-Rouen. The petrol-powered car won

After 1903, races were held at race tracks or 'circuits' instead of on roads. The world's first official motor-racing circuit was Brooklands in England

The 'Grand Prix' race was started in 1905 by the French

There are now many Grand Prix races, in places like Malaysia, Australia, Canada and Germany

HISTORY OF MONZA

Monza, or Autodromo Nazionale Monza, is the third oldest motor-racing track in the world. It was built in 1922

The track is named Monza after the town where it's located. Monza is in northern Italy

Monza is one of the fastest circuits in the Grand Prix. Drivers can reach speeds of up to 225 miles per hour

The Italians call Monza 'La Pista Magica' or 'The Magic Trick'

SECRET AGENT GADGET INSTRUCTION MANUAL

Camera Shades: When you need to take photos of someone or something, use the GPF's Camera Shades. Camera Shades look like ordinary sunglasses but are actually a hi-tech digital camera. Just touch the sensor on the top right of the frame to take a picture. Photos can be wired directly to your Watch Phone or can be downloaded from a memory chip hidden inside the frame.

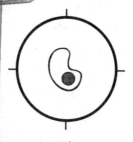

Big Ears: When you need to listen in on a secret conversation, place one of these transparent sticky balls on a person's body. Its hi-tech amplifier will pick up even the slightest sound and send whatever is said into a separate recording device. Perfect when you need to capture a crook admitting to something terrible.

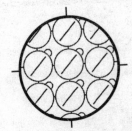

Anti-G Tablets:

The GPF's Anti-G tablets help keep secret agents' bodies working normally when they're travelling at high speeds. Just swallow one of these grey tablets to stop you from passing out. The effect of one tablet lasts up to two hours.

Torpedo: With the push of a button, this lunch-box-sized container transforms into a torpedo-shaped rocket capable of travelling more than 200 miles per hour. Just hop on the seat, grab onto the handles and wait for its hydrogen jets to fire up. Make sure you're wearing your protective gear (goggles and helmet) before setting off. If you're travelling at speeds greater than 100mph, you'll need to take an Anti-G tablet (see above).

Chapter 1:
The Championship

CRASH!

Jack felt his body jolt backwards and then forwards. He'd been hit from behind.

'I'm going to get you for that!' he yelled to his friend Richard. Richard had just slammed into Jack with his go-kart, sending him into an inflatable barrier.

'Not if you can't catch me!' Richard yelled as he leaned forward onto his steering wheel and cruised past Jack.

Jack and Richard were in their friend Charlie Abbott's back garden celebrating his tenth birthday. Because it was a Saturday, Charlie's parents had hired three go-karts for an hour of fun-filled racing. Richard, Jack and Charlie were competing against each other to see who would win the Abbott Family Go-Kart Grand Prix.

Jack put his foot on the accelerator, but the front end of his go-kart was stuck. The marshal jumped over and pushed Jack's go-kart back on course. Turning his wheel gently to the right, he aimed for the corner ahead.

BANG!

Jack side-swiped Charlie, who was trying to get by on the inside.

'Sorry!' Jack smiled slyly as he sped away in hot pursuit of Richard.

'You dog!' yelled Charlie, trying to catch up.

As Jack rounded the corner, he could
see Richard ahead. Richard was looking
over his shoulder at Jack, and he didn't
see another barrier in front of his kart.

BOING!

Richard's kart bounced into the soft
barrier. In the time it took for the marshal
to help Richard out, Jack had come up
alongside him. Now the two boys were
neck-and-neck.

Jack put his foot down and willed his go-kart to cross the line first. When it did, it was by a hair. Jack was the winner of the Abbott Family Grand Prix! The entire party cheered and whistled.

At the 'official' award ceremony, Jack, Charlie and Richard stood on the podium that Charlie's dad had made and accepted their medals.

'Lucky break,' said Richard, looking up at Jack from the block just below.

As Jack accepted his gold medal, he
looked down at the foil-wrapped
medallion. He knew there was a delicious
disc of milk chocolate inside.

Climbing down, the boys found a spot
on the grass and opened their treats. As
Jack sat there with Richard and Charlie, he
thought about how much fun he was
having and how much he liked hanging
out with his friends.

'Time to get going,' said a voice from across the garden. Jack looked up. It was his dad walking towards him.

Jack licked the chocolate off his fingers. 'OK,' he said as he stood up and turned to his friends. 'See you at school on Monday, guys.'

'See ya,' said Richard.

'Later,' said Charlie, lifting his hand.

'Happy birthday!' said Jack. He slapped his hand into Charlie's before walking over to join his dad.

Jack and his father thanked Mr and Mrs Abbott for the fun afternoon. Climbing into the back seat, Jack was still glowing with delight as his dad started the engine and the two of them drove away.

Chapter 2:
The Fanatic

As soon as Jack got home, he walked through the kitchen and past the table where his mum left the post.

Excellent! thought Jack when he spied a parcel in the shape of a magazine that was addressed to him. It was *Fast Cars*; the number one magazine for fans of the Grand Prix racing competition, and one of Jack's favourites.

Ever since Jack was young, he'd had a thing for cars. As soon as he could walk, he'd toddle over to the front window and watch them speed down the road. At one-and-a-half years old, he was asking his parents to read his dad's car magazines to him. Not surprisingly, one of Jack's first words was 'Maserati'.

His brother, Max, loved cars too and they used to argue over which car was the most beautiful. As Jack and Max grew older, they became interested in other things like football and swimming, but they never lost their passion for cars.

Secretly, Jack longed to become a racing-car driver, just like his hero, Morgan Parks. Morgan Parks was one of the youngest racing-car drivers on the Grand Prix circuit. From the time Morgan was nine, he was winning local go-kart races, and by fifteen had won the World Go-Kart Championships. Now that he was twenty, he was old enough to drive in a Grand Prix. And not for just any racing team, but for the Italians.

Morgan had become so good that he was close to winning his first World Championship. All he had to do was beat the previous year's winner, Kurt Weber, in the upcoming Grand Prix at Monza, in Italy. The world was holding its breath to see if he could do it.

In fact, Morgan was on the cover of this month's *Fast Cars* magazine. Inside was a story telling the readers what they needed to know about him and the Monza Grand Prix. By now all Jack could think about doing was getting upstairs, finding somewhere comfy to sit and reading all of the juicy details.

Chapter 3:
The Destination

As Jack carried his magazine upstairs, he glanced at Max's room on the way and wondered if his brother, wherever he was, was thinking about the race too.

Jack closed his bedroom door behind him, lay on his bed and got comfortable. Opening his magazine to page eighty-two, he began to read through the life story of his racing hero.

Just as he was getting to the bit about the weekend's race, a familiar sound came from over his left shoulder. He looked over to his bedside table, and there was his magical globe, Whizzy, spinning wildly. It was 7:30 p.m.

'Ahem!' Whizzy coughed and spat out a jigsaw piece.

Jack quickly closed his magazine, leaving it on the bed, and leaped onto the floor. He picked up the piece, which was in the shape of a boot.

Most countries, as far as Jack could tell, didn't have a special shape. But this country did. There was only one country in the world that looked like a boot, and that was Italy.

Bellissimo! thought Jack, who had been to Italy before and loved it. His parents had taken him and Max there once when they were younger.

Walking over to his Magic Map, Jack put the piece where it belonged. Almost instantly, the name 'ITALY' appeared and

then vanished. Jack quickly went back to
his bed and pulled out his Book Bag.

He tapped his Watch Phone and asked it for the code of the day. When the GPF sent back the word T-O-M-A-T-O, Jack nearly laughed out loud. He opened the bag, making sure that he had all his gadgets. Inside were his Camera Shades, Voice-Capture Device and the Torpedo. As he closed his bag and threw it over his shoulder, he stepped towards the Magic Map. The purple light inside Italy was glowing now.

When the time was right, Jack yelled, 'Off to Italy!' Then the light flickered and burst, swallowing him into the Magic Map.

Chapter 4:
The Surprise

When Jack arrived, it was daytime and he
was seated in a massive grandstand.
Down below was an enormous racing
track. All around him were men, women
and children, mostly dressed in red.
Across the way, some spectators held up
a red flag. Jack's eyes widened. It was the
flag of the Italian racing team. As Jack sat
there, the crowd started to chant.

'*La Pista Magica!*'

'*La Pista Magica!*'

From the stories in *Fast Cars* magazine,
Jack knew that *La Pista Magica* meant
'The Magic Track'.

As he was trying to figure out whether
he was on a mission or in the middle of a
dream, a loud noise ripped through the
air from below.

VAROOOM!

Quickly, Jack looked to see a Grand Prix racing car speed by in front of the stand.

He blinked a few times. Is this for real? he thought.

VAROOOM!

A red flash of colour flew by. The crowd went wild. They stood up and began to cheer.

'Morgan!'

'Morgan!'

It was his hero.

VAROOOM!

Another speeding car raced by. This time it was silver. It was the German driver.

Jack sat there, stunned. There was no way he was this lucky. But looking around at the stands, the people and the cars, there was no way he was anywhere else. Jack was the luckiest boy alive. He was sitting in the grandstand at one of the most famous racing tracks in the world. Jack was at Monza watching the practice lap before tomorrow's Grand Prix.

Chapter 5:
The Introduction

Just then, Jack felt something tickle his ear. He thought he could hear somebody whispering to him from behind.

Carefully, he looked over his shoulder. Sitting behind him was a man wearing a navy-blue suit and expensive sunglasses. Behind the shaded lenses, Jack could see the man's eyes nervously darting all over the place.

'Come with me,' he said softly as he placed his hand on Jack's shoulder.

Jack pulled away. He didn't like it when strangers touched him.

'Come with me,' the man said again. From his accent, Jack could tell that he was Italian.

'Why should I?' said Jack, who decided it was a good idea to be cautious.

'Because I'm the one who called the GPF,' said the man. Before Jack could respond, he carried on. 'Sorry to seem so serious,' he said, leaning a bit closer. 'But I need to be careful. My name is Roberto Panini.' Putting his hand out to Jack, he added, 'I'm the boss of the Italian team.'

Jack gulped as he shook Mr Panini's hand. He couldn't believe he'd been called in by the head of one of the most famous motor-racing teams in history. Jack didn't recognize him with his sunglasses on.

'What can I do for you?' he asked as he looked at the man. Roberto was about fifty-five, with mostly black hair, except for some silver streaks.

'Not here,' said Roberto. 'There are too many people,' he added, looking around. 'We need to find a place to talk.'

Jack looked around too. Although most of the fans were focused on the track, you could never be sure who was listening in on conversations, especially in crowds.

'Come with me,' Roberto said, standing and motioning for Jack to follow him out of the viewing area.

VAROOM!

Another racing car screeched by. This time, Jack recognized it as one of the French team's cars.

Roberto climbed the steps and disappeared from view. Jack followed and found himself at the top of a large walkway that wound itself around the stadium. Roberto and Jack walked the entire length and down another flight of stairs until they were on the ground.

Moving quickly, Jack followed Mr Panini through the crowds and towards a grassy area to the right. When he got to a lone tree, Roberto stopped and turned to Jack.

He took his sunglasses off. 'The reason I have called you here today,' he said, getting to the point, 'is that I think someone is trying to hurt my star driver.' As if Jack didn't know who that was, Roberto added, 'Somebody is trying to eliminate Morgan Parks.'

Chapter 6:
The Cover

'What?' said Jack, who was completely stunned. He couldn't believe anyone would think of harming another person, let alone his racing idol.

Mr Panini let out a big sigh. 'During a routine check this morning, our chief engineer found a faulty brake pipe in car number one,' he explained.

Jack knew that Morgan drove car number one; Manuel Garcia drove car number two. He also knew that the brakes on all cars worked because of pressure put on the brake pads by fluid inside the brake pipes.

If the brake pipe was broken, the fluid would leak out, causing the brakes to fail. In a car driving 200 miles per hour, that would spell disaster for a driver like Morgan Parks.

'How do you know that someone tampered with it?' Jack asked. 'Is it possible that it could have cracked on its own?' He pretty much knew the answer to that question, but he had to ask it anyway.

Roberto looked at Jack. 'Absolutely not. Plus, the pipe looked like someone had bashed it with something. I can't have Morgan hurt before tomorrow's race,' he said. 'I need you to figure out who did this and make sure they don't try it again.'

'What makes you think they will?' asked

Jack, figuring that once their plan failed the first time they might not want to risk getting caught the second.

'There's too much riding on this race not to,' said Roberto.

Jack agreed. Morgan was about to lead the Italians to this year's championship. With Morgan out of the picture, it would make way for another team to grab the title.

'The best way for me to work out who's behind this,' offered Jack, 'is to go undercover.'

Roberto was listening carefully. 'What do you suggest?'

'Why don't I pretend that I'm a reporter for *Fast Cars* magazine?' Jack said.

He decided he knew enough about the magazine to pretend that he worked for them. 'Let's say I'm doing a story called "Twenty-four Hours Before the Race",' he added. 'You've granted me unlimited access to the cars, crew and drivers so that I can write about what it's really like behind the scenes.'

Jack carried on, 'It's a perfect way for me to interview and observe everyone involved without anyone catching on. And if we're lucky, the person who did it might forget I'm there and slip up.'

'I like your thinking,' said Roberto, nodding his head. He seemed pleased with Jack's ideas.

'But before I begin,' said Jack, 'I'd like to get an idea of who you think is behind this.'

Roberto's eyes scanned the field. 'It could be anyone,' he said, letting out another big sigh. 'It could be a member of my crew, another driver, a sponsor . . . anyone.'

'Have you said anything to Morgan?' asked Jack.

'No,' said Roberto. 'The only person who is aware that something happened is the chief engineer. Speaking about Morgan,' he added, 'I need him to stay focused. When we discovered the brake pipe had been damaged, we had to give him the number two car. We told our workers it was due to "technical problems" on Morgan's car.'

'Don't worry,' said Jack, trying to reassure Mr Panini. 'I'll find out who's responsible. I'm a big fan of Morgan and the team,' he added.

'Good,' said Mr Panini, looking a bit more relaxed. 'I asked for someone who knew about cars.' He smiled at Jack. 'Here's my business card with my mobile number on it. We'll need to keep this conversation between us,' he added.

Jack reached into his Book Bag and pulled out his Morphing Badge. The Morphing Badge was a plastic badge tied to a thin chain. It had a near-invisible keyboard on the other side that a secret agent could use to programme information. Whatever he or she typed would appear on the front, next to the picture of the secret agent that was already there.

Jack quickly typed in:

 PRESS PASS

FAST CARS MAGAZINE

Name: Jack Stuart

When the badge was finished, Jack put the chain around his neck. 'Ready,' he said.

'Fantastic,' said Roberto, putting his sunglasses back on. 'Now, let me take you to the crew.'

Chapter 7:
The Star

They left the tree and followed a path up some steps, across a bridge and over the circuit until they reached the ground on the other side.

When Jack entered the 'pit garage' – the room where the team, drivers and the cars were – he noticed that Morgan had just pulled in after finishing his qualifying lap. He had the second fastest time of the day, which meant that later on he'd get a chance to race for pole position. Pole position meant the first car to start in the next day's race.

'Great lap, Morgan!' said one of the team members, tapping Morgan on the helmet as he climbed out of the car. He was dressed head-to-toe in the Italian team's famous red racing suit.

Jack stood and watched as Morgan took off his helmet. Underneath was a fire-proof material that covered his wavy brown hair. Then he took off the Head and Neck Support plate, or HANS, which sat behind his neck to protect it in case of an accident.

He tried not to be, but Jack was star-struck. Here he was in the same room as

one of the greatest drivers of all time.

'Fantastic job, Morgan,' Roberto said
to his driver, giving him the thumbs-up.
'Let's see if we can get pole.' Then
Roberto quickly changed the subject
to address the crew. 'This is Jack Stuart,
everyone. He's a junior reporter for
one of my favourite magazines,
Fast Cars.'

Everyone in the box went quiet and looked at Jack.

Roberto carried on, 'As a favour to my friend, the editor, I've agreed to let him be a bit of a "fly on the wall" over the next twenty-four hours. He'll have unlimited access to all of you and the cars. Just go about your business and pretend he's not here,' he said. 'But when you see him, make sure you treat him well.'

With that, Roberto patted Jack on the back and left him standing at the front of the room. He had a feeling the crew was wondering what to do with a nine-year-old kid.

'Hey there!' said a voice from the side. Jack was too deep in thought to realize it was Morgan Parks making his way over.

'So,' he said, looking at Jack's badge, 'you work for *Fast Cars*?'

Jack stammered a bit and then gathered himself. He looked up at the twenty-year-old. 'Sure do,' he said as he put out his hand. 'It's great to meet you. I'm a really big fan.'

Morgan laughed and shook Jack's hand. 'That's what they all say. That is, until I lose. And then somebody else will have my fans.'

Jack couldn't help but like Morgan. He seemed like a great guy. 'Do you think I could interview you later?' Jack asked. He thought it might be a good idea to look for any information that might lead to a possible suspect.

'Sure,' said Morgan. 'How about after the next qualifying round? I'll have a few minutes then.'

'Great,' said Jack, feeling pretty excited.

'You know,' Morgan said, looking at Jack, 'I was about your age when I started karting.' It looked as though he was thinking about some happy memories. 'Well,' he said, remembering where he was, 'I'd better get going.'

Morgan walked off, leaving Jack at the front of the room. The crew was busy swarming over his car, checking the engine's on-board computer and the driver's statistics from the qualifying lap.

Now, Jack figured, was the perfect time to watch the people who had the most contact with the car and the biggest opportunity to hurt Morgan Parks.

Chapter 8:
The Pit Garage

From what Jack could tell there were two kinds of people there – the engineers and the mechanics. The engineers were responsible for designing the car and watching its progress during the race. The mechanics were there to fix any problems and keep the car in good working order. From what Jack could tell there were eight of each, making sixteen people (and sixteen suspects) in the garage with access to Morgan's car.

Jack watched each of them carefully as they worked on the car. From what he could see, there wasn't anything strange about what they were doing.

Just then, Jack heard some high-pitched clicking over his right shoulder. He quickly turned to see a row of photographers taking pictures from outside.

'Morgan!' one of them yelled, trying to get his attention. When Morgan turned to pose for the man, dozens of flashing lights went off.

'Thanks!' yelled another as the crew of photographers moved on to the Japanese pit garage, which was next door.

When the photographers had cleared, Morgan turned to chat to the chief engineer, who had a special badge on his suit.

As the two men were speaking, the famous movie star Hugh Perry and his friends strolled in. Jack knew who it was because he was known for collecting expensive cars. He brushed by Jack, not taking any notice of him, and made his way over to Morgan. Morgan greeted Hugh by shaking his hand and giving him a hug.

After a few quick words where the actor wished Morgan 'Good luck, man', he and his crowd turned and left.

Then, as if Morgan hadn't had enough visitors, Jack heard another voice that sounded familiar. It had a German accent. Jack turned to see who it was. It was Kurt Weber, the lead driver for the French. He was wearing his team's signature light-blue racing suit.

Jack knew it was common for the driver and the maker of his car to be from different countries. Kurt was a German driving a French car; Morgan was British driving for an Italian team.

'My friend!' Kurt said, walking over to
Morgan with his arms outstretched.
Morgan's reaction, although polite, told
Jack that Kurt wasn't one of his mates.

'What's up, Kurt?' asked Morgan, keeping it short.

'So sorry to see you in second place,' said the German, who spoke as though his jaws were wired shut. 'I guess I'm running a bit quicker than you today.'

'Yeah,' said Morgan, faking a smile. 'I guess.'

'Well,' said Kurt, 'see you over my shoulder in the next round.' He spun on his heels and left the garage.

'That guy is so annoying,' said Morgan, turning to the chief engineer. 'The reason I came second was because he squeezed me out at the last corner.'

'Sparky!' yelled another voice passing by the garage. Jack knew that 'Sparky' was one of Morgan's nicknames.

Morgan looked at the door, but this time a smile spread across his face. Jack recognized the driver walking in. It was

Carlos Gomez, the Spanish driver for the German team. Jack had read that Morgan and Carlos were friends.

After a quick chat, Carlos left Morgan, who began to put on his helmet for the next qualifying round.

When he and the car were ready, Morgan climbed in. The team pushed the car out of the garage and onto the side road. He started the car and revved its ten-cylinder engine.

VAROOM!

Once the crew had completed the final checks, Morgan tore off down the track and waited for the last of the qualifying laps to start. Driving in just under 1 minute and 21 seconds, Morgan set a new track record and, to everyone's delight – other than Kurt Weber's – snatched the next day's pole position out of the French team's hands.

Chapter 9:
The Press Conference

Afterwards, Jack heard some of the crew talking about a 'press conference'. He followed Morgan and the crew from the pit garage, over the track and into a tall building made of glass. This was the Monza Media Centre, and it was where reporters and photographers got a chance to ask the drivers questions before the next day's big race.

Because Morgan had driven the fastest time of the day, he got to sit in the middle of the table at the front of the room. On either side of him were some of the other drivers.

As Jack took his place at the back, he stood there thinking about his secret identity. It was perfect. Being a reporter gave him the chance to observe an entire room of suspects – from the drivers to the

JAKE   CARLOS   MORGAN

owners, they were all there. And because he was such a fan, he recognized nearly everyone.

Seated at the driver's table were: Jake, from the American team; Carlos, from the German team; Morgan, from the Italian team; Kurt, from the French team; and Marcus, from the Japanese team.

KURT   MARCUS

Since anyone in the room could be a suspect, Jack grabbed his Voice-Capture Device, or VCD. This small yellow box could record a speaker's voice and tell you if he or she were a criminal. Knowing that most crooks didn't stop at one crime, Jack figured that if there was a bad guy in the room, there was a chance that he or she could be involved in tampering with Morgan's car.

As he lifted the small yellow box, a voice boomed across the room. 'This press conference is about to start!' The crowd quietened down. The first reporter asked his question.

'So,' he said, 'Morgan, can you tell us why you're using Manuel's car in tomorrow's race? After all, we know it's your team's number two.'

'Well,' said Morgan, leaning into the microphone, 'my usual car has "technical

difficulties" and the engineers and
mechanics are looking into the problem.'

'How confident do you feel about

winning?' said another, directing his question to Morgan.

'Pretty confident,' Morgan replied, smiling.

Jack took a look at the VCD. There was no flashing light going off, which meant Morgan was as honest as Jack thought.

'What about you, Kurt?' said a female reporter, who said she worked for the *Monza News*.

'Well, you know,' he answered, 'I have felt confident all along that we will defend our title. Whatever it takes,' he added, grinning at the audience.

Jack glanced at the gadget again. The small red light on the top was flashing now. He punched a few buttons and downloaded the information. There was a screen to the right of the light. It read:

```
KURT WEBER

^

ARRESTED AT 16 YEARS OF AGE
FOR STEALING AND JOYRIDING IN
CARS

^

ARREST DETAILS KEPT FROM
PUBLIC DUE TO JUVENILE STATUS
```

Although Kurt had been in trouble a long time ago, Jack thought it was interesting that the crime involved tampering with and stealing a car.

'Marcus,' said a female reporter from *Race* magazine, 'you're fourth in the standings. How will that affect your driving tomorrow?'

'Like I have nothing to lose,' he replied.

Jack thought his comment was interesting. He looked down at the VCD.

It was flashing red again. When Jack
downloaded the information, he was
surprised to see the result.

MARCUS CHARLES

^

ARRESTED AT 15 YEARS OF AGE
FOR STEALING AND JOYRIDING IN
CARS

^

ARREST DETAILS KEPT FROM
PUBLIC DUE TO JUVENILE STATUS

Jack's eyes widened. As crazy as it
seemed, he began to wonder whether
Kurt or Marcus or both could be involved
in damaging Morgan's car. After all, they
had similar arrest records and they
obviously knew their way around cars. The
team bosses who hired them wouldn't
have known about their past histories

because their records had been sealed.

'Mr Slater,' said an unknown reporter to a member of the audience, 'what will it do to your sponsorship of the French team if they don't win the title this year?'

The spotlight flashed onto a man sitting in the second row. He was wearing a cream-coloured suit. There was nothing unusual about him except for his nose, which was crooked, and the flashy watch on his left wrist, which Jack knew cost a lot of money.

Jack recognized him as the president of Fizzy Pop, one of the world's most popular soft-drink brands. Fizzy Pop was sold everywhere from London to Thailand – they were huge.

Because Fizzy Pop sponsored the French team, Jack thought it was a fair question. After all, the sponsors were the ones who had the most to lose. They gave millions to the racing teams to win these championships, and in return the teams became moving advertisements for their brands. Jack was interested in what he had to say too.

Mr Slater cleared his throat. 'We are proud sponsors whatever happens tomorrow.'

Jack looked at his VCD. Nothing showed up. Mr Slater was 'clean'.

After Mr Slater had finished speaking, someone called across to the drivers that the press conference was over. They stood up and began to walk out, one by one. Jack might not be a real reporter, but he thought the press conference was very helpful. After all, he'd gathered some interesting information.

Chapter 10:
The Interview

After the press conference, Jack caught up with Morgan back at the pit garage. He was alone, checking up on his gear.

'Hi, Morgan,' said Jack, trying not to surprise him from behind.

'Hiya, kid,' he said, spinning round.

'Is it all right if I interview you now?' asked Jack.

'Sure,' said Morgan. 'I'm pretty much finished with my set-up for tomorrow.' He perched himself on a tall chair next to where he was standing.

'So, tell me,' Jack started, 'how do you rate your chances for tomorrow?' He felt a bit silly asking the same question as the other reporters, but he needed Morgan to think he was for real.

'Pretty good, I think,' he said. 'As long as Kurt plays fair, I'll have a clear shot at the title.'

Jack agreed with that statement. 'On that note,' he asked, 'can you tell me a bit about Kurt and Marcus Charles, the driver for Japan?' He thought it might be interesting to find out more about those two from someone who knew them.

'Just that they came through the ranks like I did,' Morgan explained. 'Except they were ten years earlier. Kurt was the fastest go-kart racer in the world,' he explained, 'until I finally broke his record at the Go-Kart Championship.'

'Kurt must have been pretty annoyed,' said Jack, who couldn't help but notice a similarity with this year's Grand Prix. Morgan was about to knock Kurt from his first-place perch again. That would give Kurt a possible motive.

'Yeah,' he said. 'I'm sure he was. But you can't stay on top for ever. You have to expect that sooner or later you're going to be replaced. He had his fifteen minutes of fame. And now,' he added, 'I guess I have mine.'

Morgan looked at his watch. 'Well,' he said, looking at Jack, 'I have to get some sleep.'

'Of course,' said Jack, who knew racing-car drivers needed as much sleep as possible. Morgan waved goodbye to Jack and closed the door behind him.

Jack sat there, alone in the pit garage. He glanced over at Morgan's car. Figuring this was a good time to check it out, he began to walk towards it. But as he did so, he heard some loud whispering on the other side of the door. In case it had something to do with the case, he decided to hide and listen for clues.

Quickly, Jack grabbed his Klimbing Kit out of his Book Bag. On the side of its circular case was a hatch that released a

powerful nylon rope for climbing. Jack
opened the hatch and pointed the
opening towards the rafters on the ceiling.
As soon as he pushed the 'eject' button,
the rope shot out and twirled around one
of the steel beams.

Jack had to hurry. The voices were getting louder and someone was turning the door knob.

He tugged on the rope to make sure it was secure. Using the strength in his arms, he pulled himself upwards, scrambling towards the beams. As soon as he reached the top, he yanked the cord back into its case, just as two people entered the room.

Chapter 11:
The Fall

When Jack looked down, he saw Kurt Weber and Marcus Charles. Quickly, he flicked on the recording feature on his VCD. He wanted to capture them speaking in case they admitted to something.

'Now, let's fix this for good,' sniggered Kurt. 'I'm sick of this guy always getting in our way.'

'Yeah,' said Marcus. 'I don't know how they found the crack in the pipe. But there's no way they're going to see this one coming.'

As Marcus was speaking, Jack spied Kurt plugging a wire into a socket behind the driver's seat. This was where the engine management computer was kept.

'A few more instructions,' said Kurt, punching some commands into a handheld device at the other end of the wire, 'and the throttle will stay open until . . . *KABOOM!*' Kurt opened his fingers in the air, as if he was showing Marcus the way a bomb exploded.

Jack gulped. The throttle was what controlled the speed of the engine. If it stayed open then the engine would go faster and faster until it eventually exploded. Normally, the driver and the engine management system would step in. But Kurt was doing something that meant nothing and no one would be able to shut it down.

'That should do it,' said Marcus to Kurt as Kurt removed the plug from the car. The two of them stood there grinning from ear to ear. Jack, on the other hand, was totally horrified. Although he had suspected them, he couldn't believe they could sink this low.

He had to stop Kurt and Marcus. Keeping his gaze on the two men, he reached for a gadget in his Book Bag. But as he did so, he lost his footing. Jack's legs slipped out from underneath him and

he fell sideways off the beam.
Instinctively, he grabbed onto the steel
bar with both hands but, in doing so, let
go of his VCD. The gadget fell to the floor
and smashed into hundreds of little
pieces. With all the noise, the two men
looked up.

'Well, well,' said Kurt, spying Jack's legs dangling just above him. 'What do we have here? A little snitch,' he went on, kicking the broken bits of the VCD everywhere.

The weight of Jack's body was causing him to lose his grip. He tried desperately to pull himself back up, but he couldn't.

'We can't let this kid tell anyone what we've done,' said Marcus. 'It'll ruin your chances for tomorrow, not to mention our careers and the money.'

Jack played over in his mind what Marcus had said . . . your chances for tomorrow . . . the money. Not only were they doing this so Kurt could win, but also because someone was paying them to do it. That meant there were more than two people involved in this crime.

'Looks like we'll have to take care of this little problem,' said Marcus.

Kurt jumped up and grabbed onto Jack's right foot. He pulled hard, causing Jack to tumble directly into Marcus's arms. Marcus pinned Jack's wrists behind his back and held them there.

'Let go of me!' shouted Jack as he tried to wriggle free.

'Oh no, you don't,' said Kurt. 'We're not going to let a little pipsqueak like you ruin our chances. We're going to put you somewhere where no one will find you. At least not until after tomorrow when I reclaim the title, and then no one will believe you.' He gave an evil smile.

'You're not going to get away with this!' Jack shouted.

By now, Kurt had pulled some tape out of one of the mechanics' tool drawers and ripped off a piece. He covered Jack's mouth with it to stop him from speaking. Jack tried to scream through the tape, but

trying to make a loud noise when your
lips are sealed is totally impossible.

Kurt returned to the drawers. He was looking for something else. Pulling out a long thin copper wire, he walked back over to Jack.

'If there had been rope, I would have used it,' he said. 'But this is all they've got.' He lifted it in front of Jack's eyes. 'Sorry, this is going to hurt.' He walked round behind Jack and pulled out a length of wire.

When Jack took the GPF's self-defence class, they taught him that if an attacker has you by the wrists then the best way to break free is to stamp on the top of the attacker's foot bone. Jack lifted his strongest leg and pounded down onto Marcus's foot.

'Owwww!' Marcus yelped as he let go of Jack to grab his sore foot.

Before Kurt could catch him, Jack made a break for it. He slid onto the floor and

towards the back door. But as he pulled
himself up to reach for the handle,
something crashed onto the top of his
head. It hit him so violently that the pain
made him drop to his knees.

He wasn't sure whether it was Kurt or Marcus who had come from behind. In his dazed state, he could feel his wrists being tied behind his back with that copper wire. It hurt a lot, but he didn't care. He was so dizzy that he slumped to the floor and completely passed out.

Chapter 12:
The Locker

When Jack woke up, he found himself sitting with his knees pulled up to his chest in what seemed like a very small space. Thankfully he still had his Book Bag. Kurt and Marcus probably hadn't thought to take it. But Jack had lost all his evidence when the VCD went crashing to the floor.

Although it was dark, he could feel that there were walls on all sides of his body. When he tried to push his legs outwards, he couldn't. Given how big he was, he guessed the space was almost one metre wide and about the same height. He wriggled onto his knees and tried to stand up. It felt as though he was in some sort of closet.

Instead of sitting there in darkness, Jack figured the best next step was to turn on his Everglo Light. The only problem was that his wrists were tied behind his

back. Luckily for Jack, when Kurt and Marcus had tied them together, they'd done it high enough so that he could still move his hands up, down and sideways.

Stretching one of his fingers over to his Watch Phone, he activated his Everglo Light. A bright glow lit up the space. It looked like he wasn't in a closet after all, but in some sort of steel locker.

Excellent, Jack thought. Although he'd just been attacked by two criminals, it was still a good day. They might have tied his wrists together, but he could reach his Melting Ink Pen. It was the only gadget that could eat through steel and it was just within reach at the side of his Watch Phone.

He used one finger to eject it, and another two to grab hold. Then, with his fingers, he twisted the top of the pen. Rubbing the pen back and forth over the copper wire, he waited for it to do its magic. When he heard a small snap, he knew he'd broken free.

As he brought his wrists round, he realized they were sore. The wire had cut into his skin and it was almost bleeding. Reaching into his Book Bag, Jack grabbed his Fix-It Tape. He peeled off two strips and wrapped one around each wrist.

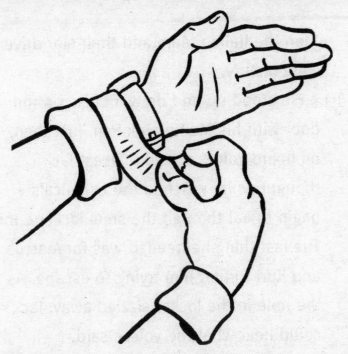

The special formula in the tape instantly
made his skin feel better.

Now that his hands were free, he had
some work to do. He had to get himself
out of this locker. Not only was he running
out of fresh air, he was also worried
about Morgan Parks. If Jack had been in
there as long as he thought, there was a
chance he'd missed the race. And if what
Kurt had done to Morgan's car worked,

then the Italian team and their star driver were history.

He stood up and drew a circle on the door with his Melting Ink Pen. Just then, he heard voices outside. Yikes! Jack thought as he watched the chemicals begin to eat through the steel locker door. The last thing he needed was for Marcus and Kurt to find him trying to escape. As the hole in the locker sizzled away, Jack could hear what the voices said.

'How's your guy doing?' said the first voice. It was an American man. Although Jack was relieved, he couldn't very well ask for help. For all he knew, one or both of these guys could be involved in the plot to hurt Morgan.

'Great,' said the second. 'It's the thirty-fifth lap and Jake's in fifth place. We swapped wings to help the downforce. It seems to be working.'

Thank goodness, Jack thought. From what he could tell, the race was still going on. Since the man didn't mention it, he figured Morgan's car hadn't exploded yet. Jack still had some time.

'We've done the same on Carlos's car,' said the second voice. 'The track is running pretty fast.' Jack guessed it was a member of the German team. 'Carlos is having the race of his career,' the man added. 'Fourth position, and only three seconds behind Marcus.'

Jack heard what sounded like running taps. Then he heard a hand drier before a door closed and everything was silent. The two men must have left the room. When the chemical from the pen had eaten through the steel, Jack punched through it and a circle of metal popped out onto the floor.

Crawling out of the locker, he noticed that he was in some sort of men's changing room. He hoped it wasn't too far from the Italians' pit garage. Jack had to get to them to stop the race – Morgan Parks' life depended on it.

Chapter 13:
The Problem

Jack rushed through the changing room and made his way outside. From what he could tell, he was at the other end of the circuit, far away from the Italian team.

VAROOM!

The cars were whizzing around furiously. Across the track and over in the grandstands, the crowd was going wild. Jack looked quickly at the scoreboard and noticed that Morgan was in first place. He was now on lap forty, which meant he had only thirteen to go.

It looked like Morgan wasn't returning to the pits again. He'd already made his two stops. Jack knew the Italians had a plan of stopping no more than twice to change tyres and refuel. Jack's only hope was to call Mr Panini so that he could radio Morgan in the car and warn him.

But when he dialled Mr Panini's number there was no answer.

Drat, thought Jack. Morgan was out there all alone. He had to do something. But catching a racing car at Monza is a tricky thing. Unless you have the Torpedo, that is, in which case it's not only easy, it's fun.

Chapter 14:
The Rocket

Jack unzipped his Book Bag and pulled out a torpedo-shaped canister about the size of a lunch-box. He placed it on the ground and pushed a few buttons on his Watch Phone. The Torpedo opened from the middle and a seat big enough for two people to sit on popped out.

He then pushed another button and the nose of the canister grew, as did the tail. At the same time two handles came out of the front and hydrogen powered jets burst from the back.

Reaching into his Book Bag, Jack pulled out his Anti-G tablets.

The GPF's Anti-G tablets helped to protect an agent's body when they were riding on something super fast. After popping a few in his mouth, Jack put on a transparent, soft hat that hardened almost immediately. He then placed his Anti-Detection Visor over his eyes to protect them from flying debris.

Normally, the Anti-Detection Visor would be transparent, but whenever a secret agent needed to hide their identity, they could change the shade from transparent to silver. That way no one could see their face.

Jack did just that, since he knew there were lots of TV cameras around. He turned on the ignition and sped off into the air.

Whizzing over trees and the barrier that

ran alongside the track, Jack nose-dived
towards the ground and headed straight
for the cars ahead.

ZOOM!

When the crowd noticed him on the track, Jack could hear them cheer. He thought how funny it must be to see someone whizzing around the track on a rocket.

ZOOM!

Jack blasted by Carlos, the driver for Germany. He could hear him shift down a gear as he spied Jack sailing past.

ZOOM!

He swiftly cruised by Marcus. I'll get you, Jack thought as he kept his focus on the car at the front.

ZOOM!

Next up was Kurt, who he ignored, carrying on until he came alongside Morgan. When Morgan noticed the Torpedo, he briefly turned towards Jack.

'Pull over!' Jack yelled, motioning for Morgan to get off the road. 'Get out of the car!'

But Morgan didn't respond. There was no way he could tell what Jack was saying. The noise of the engines was far too loud and the silver shade on Jack's visor was too dark for Morgan to realize that it was him. Before Jack could de-activate the Anti-Detection Visor, Morgan looked back at the road and sped off again.

'Pull over!' Jack yelled, trying to catch up. 'The car's about to explode!'

But Morgan still couldn't hear him. Jack wasn't surprised that he was ignoring him. After all, this was the biggest race of his life. Jack was going to have to think of something else – and fast – or else Morgan Parks and the Italian team were toast.

Just ahead, on the side of a bend, Jack spied a large area with small rocks on the ground. This was a gravel trap – the perfect way to bring Morgan to safety.

ZOOM!

Increasing his speed, Jack finally caught up to Morgan. He waited a moment before nudging the Torpedo Morgan's way. Reacting quickly, Morgan swerved to avoid Jack, skidding to a stop in the middle of the gravel pit.

'What on earth do you think you're doing?' Morgan screamed at Jack, climbing out of his car and shoving open his visor in anger. By now, Jack had pulled up next to the Italian car.

As Jack was about to explain the situation, he heard a horrible noise. It sounded like the engine on Morgan's car was out of control . . . It was about to explode.

'Jump on!' yelled Jack. A puff of oily smoke spat out of the car's exhaust. When Morgan saw this, he knew what was going to happen too. He leaped onto the Torpedo and sat behind Jack.

'Hold on!' shouted Jack as he flicked the handles. The two of them shot off into the distance, just as a massive explosion ripped across the track.

KABOOM!

Chapter 15:
The Flames

As Jack and Morgan sailed away from the explosion and over to the pits, they looked back at the car. One of the world's most beautiful and expensive racing cars was in the middle of a fireball. Flames were spiking towards the sky and Jack could see a fire crew speeding in the direction of the wreck.

When they got to the pit garage, Jack slowed the Torpedo down and let it hover outside. Morgan climbed down, took off his helmet and turned to Jack.

'Who are you?' he said. 'You obviously don't work for *Fast Cars*.'

'Just a kid who loves cars,' said Jack, smiling. Although it was pretty obvious that he was more than a reporter, he decided it was better to keep Morgan in the dark.

'I owe you my life,' Morgan said as he placed his hand in Jack's. 'Thank you. If you ever need anything—'

At that moment, a group of reporters and photographers appeared in the distance.

'Morgan! Morgan!' they shouted. The young driver turned towards them.

With Morgan's gaze in the other direction, Jack quickly tapped on his Watch Phone, shutting down the Torpedo. He then whipped off his hat and visor and stuffed them and the gadget into his Book Bag.

As the reporters swamped the driver, they forced him away from Jack and over to the far side of the room. Morgan looked at Jack as if to say sorry, and started answering their questions.
'What happened out there?' asked one reporter.

'Who was that who saved you?' yelled another reporter.

'Do you think the car will ever race

again?' shouted a third.

Just then, Jack heard a noise in the background. It was the crowd. Kurt had crossed the finish line in first place. He'd kept his title as reigning champion of the Grand Prix.

Now that Morgan was safe, Jack had some unfinished business to attend to. There were two drivers and at least one unknown person out there who were responsible for messing with Morgan's car. With an idea of how he could catch all three, Jack hung his press badge back around his neck, walked alongside the other reporters and made his way over to the winner's area.

Chapter 16:
The Winner

The winner's circle was a fifteen-minute walk from the pit garage – the perfect amount of time for Jack to make a few phone calls. By the time he'd arrived, Kurt and Marcus were already there, as was Carlos, who finished in third place for the Germans. Jack blended into the crowd so Kurt and Marcus couldn't see him.

Guessing that whoever hired Kurt and Marcus might try to speak to them at the ceremony, Jack plucked two clear and sticky pea-sized gadgets out of his Book

Bag. These were the GPF's Big Ears, which could pick up very quiet sounds and feed them back into a speaker on an agent's Watch Phone as well as a special recording device in their Book Bag.

Jack tossed one of the Big Ears towards Kurt, where it softly attached itself to the front of his overalls. He threw the other one towards Marcus, and it stuck to the top of his shoulder. Since there was so much commotion going on, neither the drivers nor the crowd noticed what Jack was doing. Finally, he pulled out his Camera Shades and put them on.

As Kurt and Marcus talked to their fans, Jack listened carefully. He heard Kurt showing off to some reporters about how he deserved to win the race. Marcus went on to another about his upbringing in a small town in France. Jack could hear the engineers on either side of the two drivers chatting about next year's race already.

And then, as Jack was standing there, something interesting happened. He saw Kurt's eyes glance and nod to somebody to the crowd. Jack looked in the direction of his gaze and noticed Mr Slater, the Fizzy Pop president, making his way to the front. Kurt nudged Marcus and they got up to greet him. The reporters started talking to Carlos about coming third.

When Mr Slater reached the two drivers, the conversation was short, but very interesting. Jack could hear Mr Slater speak first.

'Well done, boys,' he said.

Jack took a few digital photos by pushing a button on his Camera Shades.

'We didn't totally get rid of our competition,' said Marcus. 'I hope that won't stop us from getting the money,' he added.

So, thought Jack, Mr Slater was the

third criminal. He was the one who hired Kurt and Marcus to damage Morgan's car – and they'd been hoping to hurt him at the same time.

'Not at all,' Mr Slater said. 'The most important thing is that the French team won.'

At that point, Jack saw Mr Slater pull two pieces of paper out of his inside jacket pocket. They looked like cheques. Jack took some more photos with his Camera Shades. Mr Slater gave one each to Kurt and Marcus, then escaped back into the crowd. Jack thought it was time to

get the police involved now that he had gathered enough evidence.

At that point, an announcer began to speak.

'Ladies and gentleman, third place in this year's Monza Grand Prix goes to Carlos Gomez from the German team!' The German team of engineers and mechanics clapped furiously.

'Second place at this year's Monza Grand Prix goes to Marcus Charles of the Japanese team!' The Japanese, who thought they might only come fourth, were delighted with their second-place finish.

'And finally,' the announcer said, 'the winner of this year's Monza Grand Prix and overall winner of the World Championship is Kurt Weber from the French team!'

At that, the crowd of French supporters

went crazy. Kurt took his place on top of the stand. After they had played the German national anthem for his home country, he shook a huge bottle of champagne, uncorked it and

sprayed it all over his team mates. It was at that point that a police van screeched into the winner's arena. At least ten Italian policemen flung open the back doors and stepped out, fully armed. Jack waved his arms to attract their attention. The police chief charged through the crowd towards him.

'Here's the evidence I was telling you about,' said Jack as he handed over the recording from his Big Ears. 'This proves that Kurt Weber and Marcus Charles were responsible for damaging Morgan Parks' car. And, most importantly, for trying to hurt him.'

'This also proves,' he went on, handing over the Camera Shade evidence, 'that Mr Slater, the president of Fizzy Pop, paid them to do it.'

Those in the crowd who heard Jack gasped at the news. The police chief's eyes widened with surprise.

'*Grazie*,' he said. Then, without missing a beat, he yelled orders to his team in Italian.

Before Kurt and Marcus knew what had happened, six of the policemen pounced on them, pulled their wrists behind their backs and slapped on some handcuffs. The crowd watched in amazement.

As they were dragged through the

crowd, Kurt passed by Jack, who was still standing next to the police chief.

'You little brat!' he hissed. 'We'll get you for this!'

'Let's see how you like having your hands tied behind your back,' said Jack, pleased that he could get his revenge.

Kurt let out a growl before being shown into the back of the police van. Marcus was led in behind him and then the door was slammed in their faces.

When Mr Slater noticed the remaining policemen heading for him, he ran in the other direction. They wrestled him to the ground and handcuffed him too before putting him in the van with Marcus and Kurt. The door slammed shut a final time.

The photographers and reporters couldn't believe how lucky they were to capture a story like this. Bulbs were flashing everywhere as they tried to get a photo of the three men.

When the driver of the police van was ready, he flicked on the sirens and red lights.

Not quite the 'victory lap' of Monza they're used to, thought Jack. They'd be going away for a long time and would never get the chance to race cars again.

Chapter 17:
The Mentor

'Well done,' said a voice from behind
Jack. It was Mr Panini. He looked pleased.

'You did a great job out there,' he said.
'I can't say I'm happy about the car, but
Morgan was what was most important.
And you got rid of two of the nastiest
drivers on the track,' he added, 'and
caught a sponsor who was as crooked as
his nose. A job well done, I'd say.'

'I'm glad I was able to help,' said Jack,
who was also happy.

'You know,' said Mr Panini, 'the way

you drove that rocket out there leads me
to believe you'd be a pretty good racing-
car driver yourself.'

'Well,' said Jack, a bit embarrassed,
'I've always wanted to be one.'

'Why don't you tell your parents to give
me a call, and I'll see what I can do to
help you get there one day?' he said.

'Really?' asked Jack, who couldn't
believe his luck. Wait until Max hears
about this one, he thought.

Realizing it was time to go, Jack shook hands with Mr Panini and said goodbye. He made his way over to the grandstand and found the seat where he had arrived. Since all the spectators had left by now, it was a perfect time and place for Jack to disappear. Punching a few buttons on his Watch Phone, he yelled, 'Off to England!'

Within moments, Jack was transported home. When he arrived back in his bedroom, *Fast Cars* magazine was still in his hands. He turned back to page eighty-two and for the next twenty minutes read about his hero, Morgan Parks. Then he drifted off to sleep with a big grin on his face.